Island
~of~
Sodor

W9-BUB-280

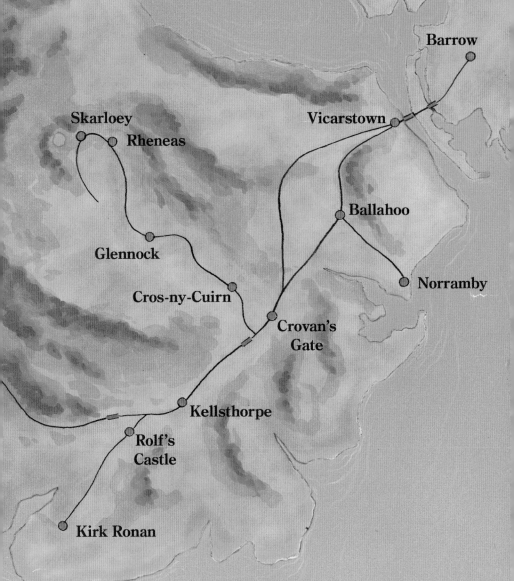

Barrow

Skarloey

Rheneas

Vicarstown

Ballahoo

Glennock

Norramby

Cros-ny-Cuirn

Crovan's
Gate

Kellsthorpe

Rolf's
Castle

Kirk Ronan

Thomas the Tank Engine & Friends™

CREATED BY BRITT ALLCROFT

Based on The Railway Series by The Reverend W Awdry.
© 2010 Gullane (Thomas) LLC.
Thomas the Tank Engine & Friends and Thomas & Friends are trademarks of
Gullane (Thomas) Limited.
HIT and the HIT Entertainment logo are trademarks of HIT Entertainment Limited.

All rights reserved. Published in the United States by Random House Children's
Books, a division of Random House, Inc., New York, and in Canada by Random
House of Canada Limited, Toronto.

Random House and the colophon are registered trademarks of Random House, Inc.

www.randomhouse.com/kids
www.thomasandfriends.com

Library of Congress Cataloging-in-Publication Data is available on request.

ISBN 978-0-375-86356-1

MANUFACTURED IN CHINA
10 9 8 7 6 5

Random House Children's Books supports the First Amendment
and celebrates the right to read.

HiT entertainment

Christmas in Wellsworth

Based on The Railway Series
by The Reverend W Awdry

Illustrated by Richard Courtney

RANDOM HOUSE New York

It was two days before Christmas. Everywhere
Thomas looked, Wellsworth was bustling with
preparations. Toby brought shoppers into town,
James pulled freight cars full of decorations, and
Henry had just delivered a large Christmas tree to
the town square.

The following night, Wellsworth would have a
wonderful Christmas Eve festival. Everyone would
gather to watch the lighting of the tree. They'd
sing carols and ring bells. Thomas couldn't wait.

"If only it would snow," he thought. "Then
everything would be perfect."

"I'm afraid we won't have a white Christmas this year," Thomas peeped as he looked up at the blue sky.

"That's okay with me," said Henry. "I have so much to do, I don't need a snowstorm now."

Thomas loved the snow, even if he had to wear his heavy snowplow. "Snow would make the Christmas Eve Festival so pretty."

Just then, Sir Topham Hatt called to Thomas.

"I have a message from Lady Hatt," he said. "She wants to come to the festival, but my car is in the garage for maintenance. I need you to run over to Kellsthorpe to pick her up. Please take Annie and Clarabel so you can bring my grandchildren as well."

"Yes, Sir!" peeped Thomas. Of all the jobs on Sodor, pulling a trainload of children was his favorite.

Thomas was soon speeding across Sodor. Everywhere he looked, people were smiling and waving. In Maron, children prepared for a Christmas pageant—with real sheep!

And as night fell, the festive lights of Rolf's Castle shined brightly. The town looked like a magic palace.

Thomas arrived in Kellsthorpe. He had made good time and was eager to make the return trip the next day.

When Thomas awoke the next morning, the weather had changed. It was cloudy and damp—and getting colder by the hour. A chilly fog rolled over the town.

Soon Lady Hatt and the children arrived at the station. They climbed aboard Annie and Clarabel, dressed in their holiday best and carrying boxes of gifts. They couldn't wait to get to Wellsworth and the festival.

The fog grew thicker. Thomas chugged away slowly.

The cold wind blew and the tracks were wet and slippery. Thomas' lamp was useless in the fog, and his Driver held the throttle tight. They crept along more and more slowly.

"This isn't very merry weather at all," Thomas peeped.

As he rolled past Rolf's Castle, Thomas couldn't see the town through the thick fog. He wanted to get to Wellsworth as soon as possible. Thomas knew they had to be careful and go slowly. He hoped they would pass through this bad weather soon.

But the bad weather didn't lift. And as it grew later and later, darkness soon added to Thomas' problems. As he climbed toward Killdane, Thomas knew he wouldn't be in Wellsworth in time for the festival. He would miss the tree lighting—and worst of all, he was sure he had ruined Christmas for Sir Topham Hatt and his family.

Meanwhile, the people of Wellsworth gathered around the tree in the town square. They lit the festive lights and sang carols, but Sir Topham Hatt was not with them.

Sir Topham Hatt waited nervously at the Wellsworth Station. There were reports of fog and frost all over the countryside. He checked his watch and worried.

"I hope everyone is okay," he whispered to himself.

Finally, as Thomas chugged over the hills outside Wellsworth, the fog lifted. He could see candles flickering in the windows of homes he passed. The streets of Wellsworth were empty, and even the sight of the great glowing Christmas tree at the center of town didn't cheer Thomas.

When they reached the station, Sir Topham
Hatt hugged his wife and helped carry the
sleeping children off Annie and Clarabel.

"And now we must get these children to bed,"
said Lady Hatt, "or Santa Claus will never arrive."

Thomas chugged back to the Yard feeling very
low indeed.

The next morning, the Yard was blanketed with beautiful snow! All the engines wished each other Happy Christmas.

"I'm sorry I missed the festival," Thomas peeped to James. "And worst of all, I think I ruined Sir Topham Hatt's holiday."

Thomas didn't know that Sir Topham Hatt was standing nearby.

"Ruined?" said Sir Topham Hatt. "You brought my family to me safe and sound, and that's the best gift of all! Taking your time in that terrible weather was the right thing to do. Thomas, I'm glad you're such a Really Careful Engine!"

Thomas was delighted.

"I am so grateful for my railway," Sir Topham Hatt announced, "I'm giving each of you a hopper full of the best coal to thank you for a wonderful year."

All the engines tooted happily.

"And, Thomas, at the request of my wife, Annie and Clarabel will be getting new seat cushions."

"It's a wonderful Christmas after all," peeped
Thomas. "And the snow did make everything
perfect."

James said *tomorrow* would be perfect.

"Tomorrow? What's tomorrow?" Thomas asked.

James laughed. "Have you forgotten Boxing Day, slowcoach?"

"Hooray! I *had* forgotten!" Thomas peeped. "More rides for children!"

Every year on the day after Christmas, all the engines on Sir Topham Hatt's railway roll out to the hospitals all over the island. Free rides and new toys and clothing are given to every child.

Boxing Day was beautiful. Thomas, James, and Henry were decorated and loaded with nice things for the children of Sodor. Then they chugged across the countryside.

Everywhere the engines went, they were met with cheering. All the children loved their presents and taking rides around the towns to see the lights and decorations.

Thomas couldn't have been happier.

"James," he called, "what's nicer than a white Christmas?"

"What?" asked James.

"A white Boxing Day!" laughed Thomas.

Can you find these things in the pictures of this story?